Hey
Cupcake

Kendra Cuzick
Pictures by Leah Cluff

DEDICATION

To Katie, Addison, Lucy, and Mabel.
My favorite cupcakes.

CONTENTS

ACKNOWLEDGMENTS

Thank you, my family, for your confidence in me. Thank you, Candice, for editing my book. Thank you, Leah, for your amazing art work. And a great big thank you to my inspiration, Katie, Addison, Lucy, and Mabel.

CHAPTER ONE

"Katie! Addie! Come quick!" Lulu called as she clumsily raced through the front door on her roller skates. She slid to a stop as Katie and Addie tumbled down the stairs to meet her. Lulu always came to visit her cousins but usually she knocked first.

"What Lulu? Did something happen?" Addie asked with concern.

"Yeah," said Katie. "What's going on?"

"Have you guys heard the news?" Lulu sputtered out of breath.

"What news?" Katie and Addie said in unison. Lulu thrust the local newspaper at her cousins as she leaned over trying to catch her breath. Older and taller Katie grabbed the paper before Addie had a chance and started reading out loud…

Baking Competition
To be held on June 12
At Sweet, Sweet Life Culinary Institute

Katie stopped reading to look questioningly at Lulu. "Baking competition?" asked the confused Katie.

"Keep reading," sputtered Lulu, who was still out of breath. Addie, reading over her sister's shoulder, continued…

The winner will receive a $100 cash prize, be featured in the Good Morning Gazette, and be awarded a personal baking session with none other than Bonnie Brown, owner of Bonnie Brown's Brownie Bakery.

"Bonnie Brown!" shouted Addie. "She's the best! I love her double fudge, salted caramel, brownies."

Katie finished reading:

Competition sponsored by Yum's Baking Supply
Participants must be registered by May 1st.

"You raced all the way here to show us this?" said
Katie.

Addie, always full of fun and adventure, asked
with wide eyes, "Lulu, are you going to enter this
baking competition?"

"I'm not going to enter the baking competition,"
said Lulu sitting down to take off her skates. "*We* are
going to enter."

"We are?!" exclaimed the sisters.

"Of course, we are," said Lulu with excitement.
"We love to bake, so why not?"

"I could give several reasons why not," Katie
said. She scooted her dog, Ruby, over and sat next to
her on the couch.

"Oh, come on Katie," said Addie. "You have our cupcake recipe practically memorized."

Lulu, who was already on the floor from taking off her skates, knelt in front of Katie and pleaded. "With Addie as our taste tester, me as the decorator, and you, with all your baking experience, how can we lose?"

"Well…" Katie said. Lulu and Addie crossed their fingers behind their backs and held their breath. "We can't leave out Mae. She might be little, but she would love to be a part of our team."

CHAPTER TWO

The three cousins, Katie, Addie, and Lulu left immediately for their youngest cousin's apartment. Addie quickly raced ahead on her bike. Lulu dashed behind on her skates. Katie followed with the wagon. Katie always pulled the wagon when going to visit Mae. It was how the girls were able to take Mae with them everywhere they went.

Being different ages didn't stop Katie, Addie, Lulu, and Mae from being inseparable. They could always be found playing at the park, swimming, riding bikes, or just hanging out at their houses. They knew each other's schedules and daily routines. They knew exactly when Mae and her mom, Aunt Leslie, got home from work and the babysitters every day.

As soon as Aunt Leslie opened the door, the girls raced in to see Mae. Addie reached her first, picking her up and spinning her around. Mae squealed and laughed with delight.

Even though Mae was only three and quite a bit younger than eleven-year-old Katie, nine-year-old Addie, and seven-year-old Lulu the older cousins loved her and made her a part of everything they did. This made Mae feel like a big girl, and she loved them for it.

When the spinning stopped the girls started talking all at once...

"Guess what Mae?!"

"You get to be a part of our team!"

"We're going to win the baking competition!"

...until Aunt Leslie spoke up. "My goodness you all have so much to say! What is it you are trying to tell us?"

"Why don't you tell them, Lulu," said Addie.

"Yeah," said Katie, "It's all your idea."

"Ok," said Lulu, turning awkwardly in her skates to talk to both Mae and her mom. "I saw this article in the Good Morning Gazette." She handed the newspaper to Aunt Leslie. "It's an advertisement for a baking competition. Katie, Addie and I are going to enter." Lulu almost fell as she knelt down in front of Mae and asked, "What do you think, Mae? Want to be on our team?"

Mae's dark eyes lit up, and she smiled big showing her bright white teeth. Then she started singing, almost shouting, "Yes! Yes! Yes!" And she did a little dance that made her curly black hair bounce.

CHAPTER THREE

"Remember how we jumped in the pool during Christmas break?" said Addie as she laid in the grass looking up at the clear blue sky.

"That was so cold!" said Katie.

"Yeah, and my mom pushed me in when I didn't jump with you," giggled Lulu.

"I can't wait for summer break so we can swim every day," Addie sighed.

"We won't have much time for swimming if we want to win this baking contest," said Katie.

Katie, Addie, and Lulu were sitting in the grass watching Mae do somersaults. After inviting her to join their team, the girls helped Mae into the red wagon and headed to the park. It was a Tuesday and a typical April day in Arizona, warm and sunny. The girls were spending as much time as they could outside before it got too hot to do anything but swim.

"We better get planning. The competition is only eight weeks away," said Lulu.

"That gives us plenty of time to plan," Addie said, then she did a somersault with Mae, getting grass stuck in her dark, silky hair.

"You two look wild with all that grass in your hair!" teased Katie.

"The competition might be eight weeks away but we have to register by May 1st. That's in one week." Lulu said more seriously.

"Ok Lu, what do we need to do to register?" asked Addie as she shook grass from her hair.

"Well, we already know we are going to make cupcakes, so we need a team name," said Lulu. "Then we need to fill out the registration form and turn it into Yum's Baking Supply by next week."

"The registration form is the easy part," Katie said as she tossed her softball up and caught it in her mitt. "The hard part is choosing a team name. We need to choose a really good name that will get everyone's attention."

The girls sat silent for a minute each thinking of the best name for their team. Lulu was picking grass out of Mae's hair when Mae said, "The Green Team!"

"That's a great name Mae," said Addie.

"Green's your favorite color, isn't it?" asked Lulu.

Mae smiled then said, "Yep, that's right. Green is my favorite color."

"I like green too Mae, but let's get a suggestion from everyone before we decide," said Katie.

"Ultra-Bakers," suggested Lulu.

"The Starlight Team," said Addie.

"The Cupcake Queens," said Katie.

"I'm not a queen," giggled Mae.

Just then Lulu's older brother, Jack, walked up and said, "Hey cupcake! Mom says it's time to come home for dinner."

"What did you say?" asked Lulu.

"Mom wants you home for dinner," said Jack.

"No, before that."

"Hey cupcake?"

"Yes! That's it!" cheered Lulu.

"What's it?" asked Katie and Addie in unison.

"Our team's name!"

"What is our team name, Lulu?" asked Mae.

"Our team name should be Hey Cupcake!"

"Yes! I love it!" said Addie.

"It's perfect," added Katie.

The girls laughed together when Mae said, "I want to be Hey Cupcake."

"I guess it's settled. Our team name will be Hey Cupcake. Thanks for the inspiration Jack," Lulu said to her brother while she stumbled to stand up on her roller skates.

"You're welcome?" said a confused Jack. "I usually don't get thanked for teasing my sister."

"Well, this time I don't mind your teasing," said Lulu. "But I will mind if you beat me home. Bye girls! I'll start filling out our registration form," she called over her shoulder as she raced Jack home.

CHAPTER FOUR

"So, what's your team name?" asked Lulu's mom, Kendra. Lulu and her mom were making cheese enchiladas for dinner. Lulu had lived in Arizona her whole life and you didn't grow up living in Arizona without loving Mexican food.

"Our team name is 'Hey Cupcake,'" Lulu's blue eyes danced with excitement as she told her mom all about her day.

"It was all Jack's idea," chimed in her oldest brother Harry.

"That's right," added Jack, "it was all my idea."

"No, it wasn't," corrected Lulu. "You were just teasing me as usual."

"Me? Tease? I never tease!"

"You do too!"

"Alright, that's enough. Harry, Jack, where's the baby?" The boys hustled to find one-year old Cal who was always into something. The boys were on Cal duty while Lulu helped with dinner. Lulu loved working in the kitchen. She had been rolling the enchiladas and stopped to lick the sauce off her fingers.

"Don't forget your hair," her mom said pointing at the red sauce in Lulu's blond hair, "and then please wash your hands again."

Lulu found the sauce in her hair then sheepishly washed her hands, again. She could never resist licking that yummy sauce off her fingers.

"So, what's the plan?" asked her mom.

"Well," said Lulu, "we have a name and we'll bake cupcakes, obviously. We just need to turn in our registration."

"Who's going to submit the registration?"

"Well, I guess I am."

"What kind of cupcakes are you going to bake?"

"I don't know…"

"What are everyone's responsibilities?"

"Ummm…"

"When are you going to practice?"

"We'll practice every day."

"Every day? Will you have time for all of that?"

"Hmmm," thought Lulu. "I think we have some more planning to do."

#

Katie and Addie were sitting at their table eating Pho. Their dad, Ott, had made the Vietnamese soup for dinner. He was actually from Laos but he spent several years of his childhood in Vietnam. Pho was a family favorite.

"Then we went to Mae's house and asked if she would be on our team," explained Addie.

"We went to the park to brainstorm and decided on a team name," said Katie.

"We're going to bake mint chocolate chip cupcakes," exclaimed Addie.

"No, we're not. Who decided that?" asked Katie.

"That's what I think we should bake. I am the official taste tester," said Addie.

"Well, I'm the head baker, I know all the recipes…"

"Alright girls," said their mom, Tera. "When do you start?"

"Tomorrow," the sisters said together.

"Just don't forget that Katie has violin tomorrow and you both have softball on Saturdays."

After dinner Katie called Lulu. "We can't practice baking tomorrow, I have violin lessons."

"Thursdays out for me, I have piano," said Lulu.

"And Saturday is softball," Addie yelled into the phone over Katie's shoulder.

"That leaves Friday. Getting together to practice baking our cupcakes might be more challenging than we thought," observed Lulu.

CHAPTER FIVE

It was Friday night and the girls were finally getting together to practice their cupcakes. With Katie's violin lessons on Wednesday, piano lessons for Lulu on Thursday and Katie and Addie's softball games on Saturday, Friday was the only day they could bake together. They each came with their own ideas.

Mae wanted strawberry cupcakes. Addie wanted mint chocolate chip. Lulu wanted red velvet. Katie wanted plain chocolate. Since Mae was the youngest they decided to make strawberry cupcakes first. They would bake each one then choose the best.

Sisters, Leslie, Tera and Kendra, closed their eyes and took a bite of their cupcakes at the same time, as the girls had ordered them to.

"Mmm," said Aunt Leslie.

"Tasty," said Aunt Tera.

"Delicious," said Aunt Kendra.

The three sisters, Aunt Leslie, Aunt Tera and Aunt Kendra, loved watching their daughters grow up together. They were more than happy to be taste testers for team Hey Cupcake.

"What do you really think?" asked Katie.

"Is it good enough to win?" asked Lulu.

"Yeah, is it good enough to win?" repeated Mae.

"I think it is," Addie said with a wink.

"I think they need chocolate covered strawberries on top as decoration," said Lulu, the team's official decorator.

"I think they need red sprinkles," said Lulu's oldest brother, Harry, staring at the pink cupcakes and licking his lips.

"We didn't ask you," said Lulu.

"We really could use everyone's suggestions," observed Katie. "People like different things and you never know what the judges are going to like."

"I guess that means we should let my brothers be taste testers too," sighed Lulu.

"Yes!" said Harry and Jack as they both reached for a soft fluffy cupcake. Baby Cal said, "Ma, ma, ma", for more, and then signed "please".

"Better give one to all of your brothers, Lulu," said her mom and she picked up Cal to put him in his high chair.

"I'm glad I don't have brothers," said Addie. "Having just one sister is bad enough!" Addie gave Katie a little push and Katie stuck her tongue out at her.

"I'd give anything for a sister," sighed Lulu.

"You don't need a sister," said Mae, "you have me!"

"That's right," said Aunt Leslie, "you have Mae!"

"And Katie and Addie," said Aunt Tera.

"You girls argue enough to be sisters," said Aunt Kendra.

"We do not!" the girls said together.

"Only sometimes," corrected Katie.

"Put that down!" shouted Lulu suddenly. "Those cupcakes are for Daddy and Uncle Ott. You've already had yours!"

Jack slowly put the cupcake he was trying to sneak back on the tray. His mom gave him a look that said, "don't try that again." Then said to everyone, "I think your strawberry cupcakes are really good. I like the idea of adding chocolate covered strawberries as decorations. But I think if you want a really fabulous cupcake, they need to be a bit moister."

"Agreed," said Aunt Tera. "The longer you bake them the drier they become so watch your baking time."

Lulu pulled out her notebook and started writing down everyone's ideas while Katie wiped up some spilled flour and Addie started piling dishes into the sink. Mae licked her fingers one more time.

"I have our registration form all filled out. We can turn it in on Monday after school," said Lulu.

"Registration is due by Tuesday, so that's perfect," said Katie.

"So, this is really happening?" said Addie excitedly.

"Yay team Hey Cupcake!" sang Mae.

CHAPTER SIX

The weeks went by and each week seemed harder for the girls to get together to perfect their baking.

"I have to practice for my violin recital," said Katie one week.

"I'm sorry girls, but Mae's sick," Aunt Leslie told them the next week.

They were able to whip up some mint chocolate chip cupcakes the next week, but the next was Katie and Addie's softball championship. With only two weeks until the baking competition, the girls were scrambling to bake Lulu's red velvet cupcakes and Katie's chocolate cupcakes. They had agreed to bake everyone's suggestions before making a final decision on what to enter in the contest but everything seemed to be going wrong. Katie spilled the milk. Addie got an egg shell in the batter. Lulu forgot to set the timer. And poor Mae was completely forgotten.

"My mint chocolate chip cupcakes were better than your plain chocolate cupcakes," Addie said to Katie.

"Mine would have been the best if you hadn't gotten egg shell in the batter and if Lulu hadn't forgotten to set the timer," accused Katie.

"I forgot to set the timer on my cupcakes, not yours, so don't blame me for your cupcakes not turning out," said Lulu.

"Well, my chocolate cupcakes are still the best and we should use them for our competition," said Katie.

"But we all have to decide," said Addie. "And I think mint chocolate chip is more original."

"I like chocolate, chocolate chip," said Mae, but nobody heard.

"We should bake my cupcakes. The cream cheese frosting from my red velvet cupcakes, is to die for," said Lulu.

"With cream cheese frosting and a strawberry on top," said Mae, but nobody heard.

"Cream cheese frosting doesn't go with mint chocolate chip," said Addie.

"We're not baking mint chocolate chip so it doesn't matter," argued Katie.

Just then Aunt Kendra walked in holding baby Cal. "How are things coming in here?" she said then froze when she saw the disaster in her kitchen. "Oh my, we have some cleaning up to do!"

"But we have to make a decision, Mom," said Lulu. "Our competition is only two weeks away."

"The first thing that needs to happen is to clean this kitchen. I'm sure by the time it's tidy you will all have calmed down and can think more clearly. Come on Mae, will you play with Cal while I help the girls?"

By the time Aunt Tera called to ask her girls to come home the kitchen was clean, the chocolate cupcakes were frosted and, on a tray, and the red velvet cupcakes were frosted and, on another tray, but the girls were still angry.

"I've made up my mind," said Katie, "I'm going to enter my chocolate cupcakes on my own, and they are going to win." She lifted her tray of cupcakes and carried them home without saying goodbye.

"We'll just see about that! Well, I'm going to enter my mint chocolate chip cupcakes, and they are going to win!" said Addie as she jumped on her bike.

"My frosting is still the best," Lulu called after them, then turned and walked to her bedroom.

Aunt Kendra was standing in her now clean kitchen wondering what had just happened when Aunt Leslie came to get Mae. "Mae's playing with Cal so I could help clean the kitchen," Aunt Kendra explained leading Aunt Leslie to the family room.

There they found Mae and Cal. Mae was quietly putting Legos together then handing them to Cal who took them and threw them in a basket.

"Hi Mae! What are you doing?" asked her mom.

"I'm making cupcakes with Cal."

"Did you bake cupcakes with the girls today?"

"No, they don't want to be Hey Cupcake anymore." Mae looked very sad.

CHAPTER SEVEN

School was out for the summer so the girls had two school free weeks of summer before the baking competition. They spent every moment not at swim team or at music lessons baking.

Katie baked and baked and baked her chocolate cupcakes so much she was sick of tasting chocolate.

Addie tried to bake her mint chocolate chip cupcakes. They tasted good but they just didn't turn out right.

Lulu's red velvet cupcakes looked amazing. She could decorate and create anything. But she soon realized her cupcakes looked a lot better than they tasted.

Mae spent all her time playing with Legos. She pretended she was baking real cupcakes when she put her Legos together. She had dozens and dozens of little colorful squares layered on each other. But Mae was sad.

"What's wrong Mae?" asked her mom.

"I can't make cupcakes," said a very sad Mae.

"These cupcakes are beautiful," said Aunt Leslie. She picked one up and pretended to eat it. "And tasty too."

"But it's not real mom. I'm not a big girl. I can't bake real cupcakes."

#

"Gross!" said Jack after he spit out the cupcake he had taken a bite of. "What's wrong with those cupcakes? They taste terrible."

"What's wrong with you?" asked Lulu. "My cupcakes are beautiful."

"They sure don't taste beautiful," mumbled Jack.

"They look delicious." Harry grabbed a cupcake and shoved it in his mouth. After chewing a moment, he gagged it down and threw the rest in the trash. "Sorry Lu, but Jack's right."

"What's wrong with me?" wondered Lulu. She offered a cupcake to her dog, Barkley. He sniffed it, then turned up his nose and walked away without eating it. "Not even Barkley will eat my cupcakes. I just can't get them right. I'm really good at decorating, but that's about it."

"I wouldn't say that, this frosting is to die for," said her dad, Damon, after licking the frosting off his finger.

"That's nice to hear, but I can't just enter plain frosting into the baking competition. What am I going to do?"

Addie looked around at the mess she had made. There was flour and cupcake batter everywhere. A tray of lopsided cupcakes sat cooling on the counter. "They taste great but the recipe is all wrong. I need Katie to help me get it just right." mumbled Addie to herself. "I've got the flavors down, but nobody will want to eat those ugly cupcakes, no matter what they taste like. If only I was good at decorating like Lulu. Nobody would be able to see how ugly they are if I could cover them with beautiful frosting."

Katie walked in the kitchen and stopped to stare at the mess. "Are you ready for the baking competition?" she asked.

"Of course, I am," snapped Addie. "Are you?"

"Of course! You know my chocolate cupcakes are perfect. Well, practically."

"Practically perfect isn't perfect," said Addie.

"Well, they will be. I just need someone to taste my next batch and then... if only I could decorate like Lulu."

"You know I could taste them for you," offered Addie.

"And then tell me the wrong thing to do to make sure I lose. No thank you!" Katie stormed off to her bedroom.

"That's not what I meant," said Addie quietly.

#

There was one week left before the competition when Aunt Tera drove the very quiet girls to swim team. Katie, Addie, and Lulu sat in the car without looking at each other. Aunt Tera and Aunt Kendra took turns carpooling to swim. Even though Mae wasn't big enough for swim team, they still took her to the pool with them. When they passed Mae's apartment without stopping to get her the girls spoke up.

"Why aren't we getting Mae, Mom?" asked Katie.

"Mae didn't want to swim today."

"Mae didn't want to? She always wants to swim," said Addie.

"Well, not today. Aunt Leslie called and said Mae is just too sad to go swimming."

"Sad? Why is Mae sad?" asked Lulu.

"Mae had her heart set on entering the baking competition, but without help she can't do it. She's just not big enough to enter on her own."

Katie, Addie, and Lulu hung their heads and didn't talk the rest of the way to the pool.

CHAPTER EIGHT

"We have one week before the baking competition. Without our help Mae can't enter," said Addie.

Katie, Addie and Lulu were sitting at the edge of the pool dangling their feet in the water. They usually spent their time before and after swim team playing in the pool. They usually spent that time swimming with Mae. But Mae wasn't with them today. She stayed home because she was sad about not being able to enter the baking competition. It was their fault she couldn't enter. It was their fault she was sad.

"You know," said Katie, "Mae's sad because of us."

"We need to make her happy," said Lulu.

"I agree," said Addie.

"What can we do?" asked Katie.

"I think we all know what we need to do," said Lulu. The girls looked at each other and nodded their heads in agreement.

After swim team Lulu put on her roller skates, Addie got her bike and Katie pulled the wagon out of the garage. Together they made their way to Mae's apartment.

"Mae, we're really sorry," said Addie.

"Yeah," said Lulu, "we weren't very nice."

"Can you forgive us?" asked Katie.

"So, we get to be Hey Cupcake again?" asked Mae hopefully.

"Yes!" the girls said together.

"We just need to decide on the cupcake we are going to bake," said Lulu.

"We all have good ideas," said Addie, "we just have to be willing to choose only one of them."

"I like chocolate, chocolate chip," said Mae, "with cream cheese frosting and a strawberry on top."

Katie, Addie and Lulu all stopped talking and stared at Mae.

"Mae! That's brilliant!" said Katie.

"Yep," said Mae. "Chocolate cupcakes for Katie. Chocolate chips for Addie. Lulu's frosting and a strawberry for me."

"Wow, Mae, I'm impressed." said Addie.

"You thought of everything," said Lulu. "You were much more thoughtful than we were. Thank you, Mae. This is really important to me. I've been wanting to enter this competition since I heard about it. I have imagined about winning ever since."

"Meeting Bonnie Brown owner of Bonnie Brown's Brownie Bakery will be so exciting. She's the best," said Addie.

"And winning $100 will be amazing. We could start our own business with that money," said Katie.

"I want my picture in the newspaper!" squealed Mae.

"Whether we win or not, entering with my best friends is what I want the most. Now, we only have one week until the competition. We better work fast and hard to get ready," said Lulu.

The girls went right to work. When they weren't eating or sleeping (or swimming) they were baking. They made dozens and dozens of chocolate, chocolate chip cupcakes. They put itty bitty chocolate chips in Lulu's cream cheese frosting. And they decorated the cupcakes with chocolate covered strawberries. With Katie's recipe, Addie's superb taste buds, Lulu's decorating, and Mae's ideas they worked together until their cupcakes were perfect. Their dads ate two, the boys ate three, baby Cal signed "more, more, more".

CHAPTER NINE

It was June 12th, the day of the baking competition. Katie, Addie, Lulu and Mae were excited. They were nervous. They were scared. They were confident. They were anxious. They knew they had a chance to win.

The girls arrived at Sweet, Sweet Life Culinary Institute with their families, wearing their favorite dresses and carrying their chocolate, chocolate chip, cream cheese, strawberry cupcakes. The sponsor of the competition, Yum's Baking Supply, was already set up. The Good Morning Gazette was taking pictures and interviewing a woman wearing a baking apron.

"Look, I think that's Bonnie Brown with Bonnie Brown's Brownie Bakery," said Addie, pointing to the woman in the apron.

"Do you think she will give us free brownies," asked Jack.

"Yeah, why don't you go ask her for some," teased Addie.

"Let's go over there, I think that is where we need to set up," Katie pointed to the long tables set up in the middle of the room.

The girls quickly found their spot to set up, the table was labeled with their team name, "Hey Cupcake".

"This is us," said Lulu. They carefully set up, placing their cupcakes on the stands they brought and added their label to the table, "Chocolate, Chocolate Chip, Cream Cheese, Strawberry Cupcakes".

"Those look delicious," said Harry. "When do we get to eat them?"

"Don't even think about it until the competition is over," said Addie.

"Don't even think about it," repeated Mae.

"Besides, haven't you had enough after all the practice cupcakes we made?" asked Lulu.

"No way," answered Jack.

"Can we look around? I want to see the competition," said Katie.

"Ooh, yes. Let's check out what everyone else baked," said Addie.

The group walked around looking at all the different goodies. They saw all kinds of baked goods, pies, cookies, cakes, brownies. They all looked amazing enough to win. They all looked so good that the girls started to feel nervous about winning.

"That cake is beautiful," Lulu stopped to look at a three-tier cake covered in butterflies made from sugar.

"Look at those," Mae pointed to a plate of chocolate covered eclairs.

"And these brownies," said Addie.

The girls were starting to feel very nervous. They kept glancing at their cupcakes, comparing them to all the other baked goods they saw.

Katie said very quietly, "My stomach is starting to hurt."

"There is nothing to worry about," said a voice. Everyone turned to see the woman wearing the apron, Bonnie Brown. "It looks like everyone here did a fantastic job. You should be proud of yourselves for entering. What is your team name?"

"Hey Cupcake," the girls said together, then giggled shyly.

"Pleased to meet you, Hey Cupcake," said Bonnie. "I look forward to tasting your cupcakes."

"They're the best," said Mae.

"They must be pretty good if you say so," Bonnie winked at Mae.

"So are your brownies," said Addie.

"Why thank you. I like them too."

Bonnie noticed the other judges heading for the judges table set at the front and said her goodbyes.

"Ok, I think the competition is getting started. Let's go sit over here girls," said Aunt Kendra.

CHAPTER TEN

Sweet, Sweet Life Culinary Institute was packed. There were tables full of the competitors' baked goods. Chairs were set up on one side of the school and were filling up fast. The three judges, a chef from the culinary school where the competition was being held, the owner of Yum's Baking Goods, and Bonnie Brown herself, sat at the front of the room at their own table.

After a few minutes one of the judges stood up and started talking in a microphone. "I am Neil Nielson, owner of Yum's Baking Goods and sponsor of this baking competition and one of our three judges." The crowd clapped politely. "Our other two judges are Debby Tener, head chef and teacher at Sweet, Sweet Life Culinary Institute and Bonnie Brown owner of Bonnie Brown's Brownie Bakery." The crowd clapped a little louder.

"Each one of our contestants has entered a baked good of their own making and they look amazing." The crowd clapped more enthusiastically. Neil Nielson continued, "We will be judging on three criteria. First, looks. How your dessert looks and presents itself is just as important as it tastes. Second, taste. We are looking for distinct flavors that have been baked perfectly. Third, uniqueness. We want something that is original, something we have never tasted before. With that being said we will start the competition!" The crowd clapped loudly.

The judges rose from their seats and headed to the tables full of all the contestants' entries. They smelled them, tasted them, looked at them from every angle, and then smelled them and tasted them again. The judges did this for each and every baked good. The crowd was silent, holding their breath in anticipation.

Katie bit her nails, Addie crossed both her fingers, Lulu shook her legs, practically jumping up and down, and Mae played with Cal, who was in his stroller, making him laugh and laugh.

The girls watched as the judges came to their cupcakes. They seemed to spend more time tasting their cupcakes than they had at the others'. They even had seconds. The girls looked at each other and smiled.

Their smiles didn't last long. When the judges came to the three-tier cake decorated in butterflies they oohed, they walked around the cake to see it from all sides, then they tasted it again.

"Oh no," whispered Addie, "I think they like that cake better than our cupcakes."

The girls grew more and more concerned as they watched the judges spend more time at three other entries. It seemed like they completely forgot about the girls' delicious cupcakes.

"I don't think we are going to win," said Lulu sadly.

CHAPTER ELEVEN

The judges stopped and talked. They pointed and wrote down notes. They walked the tables again and wrote down more notes. They stopped for a minute in front of the Chocolate, Chocolate Chip, Cream Cheese, Strawberry Cupcakes. They stopped for two minutes in front of the butterfly cake.

Finally, the judges returned to their table and announced that they would need ten minutes to discuss and that everyone was welcome to look at the baked entries one more time. Cal got grumpy and Aunt Kendra had to take him out. Mae jumped up and asked for a drink. Katie, Addie and their parents walked to the dessert tables to look again. Lulu sat in her chair. She was so nervous she felt frozen to her chair.

"Come on Lu," said Jack, "let's go look again."

"I can't. I just can't. What if we don't win? I'm so nervous!"

Lulu's dad came and sat next to her. "You're worried about not winning?" he asked. Lulu slowly nodded. "What will happen if you don't win?"

"If we don't win we lose."

"Who says you lose? Will the judges call the winner and then say, 'and the loser is…'?"

Lulu giggled and said, "No."

"Then is there a loser?"

"I guess not."

"You're right. You're not a loser and you won't be a loser. The judges might declare a winner and that winner might get a prize but think about all that you have already won just by entering."

Just then Neil Nielson asked everyone to take a seat. The judges were back at their table ready to announce the winner.

The girls ran back to their seats to sit next to Lulu. They grabbed hands and held their breath.

"We have tasted some amazing things today. Each contestant should be very proud. But we could only choose one of you to receive the cash prize, be featured in the Good Morning Gazette, and be awarded a personal baking session with our very talented Bonnie Brown owner of Bonnie Brown's Brownie Bakery. We made our judgment based on looks, taste and uniqueness. There was one entry that really excelled, Sylvia Bean, your butterfly cake was beautiful and unique. We have never seen anything like it."

The girls slumped in their seats when Hey Cupcake wasn't called. Katie, Addie and Lulu looked as if they were about to cry.

Neil Nielson continued, "We want to recognize Sylvia Bean for creating a one of a kind cake. You did a fabulous job and we applaud your efforts. However, we had one dessert that, as delicious and beautiful as everything was, outshone all the others. I am pleased to announce the winner of this year's Baking Competition…. Hey Cupcake!"

Mae jumped to her feet and shouted, "We did it! We did it!" Addie and Katie squealed and then hugged. Lulu sat in her seat. She couldn't believe her ears. She had wanted to win so badly she didn't think they would.

"Can we get team "Hey Cupcake" to come up here and get your reward? Katie, Addie, Lulu, Mae. Come on up here girls."

Mae pulled Lulu to her feet and drug her to the judges' tables. Together the girls stood looking surprised and excited and nervous. They held hands and smiled. They were too happy to do anything but smile.

The judges took turns explaining why they chose Hey Cupcake as the winner.

"Their cupcakes were soft and fluffy. Cooked to perfection."

"They were decorated beautifully. The chocolate covered strawberries nestled in that creamy white frosting was perfect."

"Out of all the cupcakes I have eaten I have never had a chocolate, chocolate chip, cream cheese, strawberry cupcake. Original and delicious."

"Let's have a round of applause for 'Hey Cupcake'".

Katie clapped. Addie threw her hands in the air. Mae jumped up and down. Lulu cried she was so happy.

CHAPTER TWELVE

"What made you decide to bake chocolate, chocolate chip, cream cheese, strawberry cupcakes?" asked the reporter.

"It was all Mae's idea," said Lulu.

"Yeah, we all wanted something different," said Addie.

"We even got in a fight because we wouldn't compromise," said Katie.

"But Mae took parts from each of our ideas and created this brand-new cupcake," said Lulu, smiling at Mae.

"That's very mature of you Mae," said the reporter. "What gave you that idea?"

"I just wanted Hey Cupcake to be together," Mae said shyly.

The girls hugged Mae and the photographer took one last picture.

#

"We won! I can't believe we won!" said Addie after they received their prize and had their interview and picture taken for the newspaper.

"Can we eat your cupcakes now?" asked Harry.

"You'll have to fight me for one first," said a voice. Everyone turned to see Bonnie Brown. "I just came to congratulate you girls. Your cupcakes were divine. We need to schedule our baking session, although you really don't need me to give you any baking tips. Maybe we can turn our baking class into you teaching me."

Everyone laughed and the parents spoke more with Bonnie Brown about scheduling the baking session. There was a line of people wanting to congratulate the girls. The boys were getting bored so they took Cal to check out the competitors' goodies in hopes of tasting a few.

Then it was all over. Hey Cupcake received their cash prize, set up a baking session with Bonnie Brown, were interviewed by the Good Morning Gazette, and loaded up the remaining cupcakes.

"That was a long day," said Jack on the way home.

Lulu looked at baby Cal who was asleep in his car seat. "It was a long day but it was a good day."

"Lu, you should be very proud of yourself," said her mom. "Not just because you won, that's an extra bonus, but because you and your cousins accomplished something very hard. You came together and worked through your differences and created something amazing to eat."

"That makes you a true winner," said her dad.

#

The next day Katie, Addie, Lulu, and Mae were sitting at the edge of the pool, dangling their feet in the water. Mae was kicking and splashing water into their faces. The cool water felt good on a hot day.

"So, what do you say girls, should we go home and bake some more cupcakes?" asked Katie.

"NO!" replied Lulu, Mae and Addie together.

"I need a baking break," said Addie.

"Me too," replied Mae.

"I think a small break is a great idea. But it can't be too long, I have big plans to use our cash prize to expand our business," said Lulu.

"Our business?" Katie and Addie asked together.

"Yes, our new cupcake baking business. Hey Cupcake is going to be huge!"

ABOUT THE AUTHOR

Kendra Cuzick enjoys cookies and a good nap. Her favorite job has been teaching preschool. She is currently going back to school for a degree in neuropsychology. Kendra lives in Phoenix Arizona with her husband and four children.

Chocolate Chocolate Chip Cupcakes
Makes 12 cupcakes

INGREDIENTS
1 stick unsalted butter

1/2 cup granulated sugar

1/2 cup light brown sugar

2 large eggs (one at a time)

3 ounces unsweetened chocolate (melted and cooled)

1 cup cake flour (sifted)

1/2 teaspoon baking soda

1/2 cup buttermilk (room temperature)

1/2 teaspoon pure vanilla extract

1/2 cup chocolate chips (semi-sweet)

DIRECTIONS
1. Cream the butter and granulated sugar and light brown sugar.

2. Add eggs one at a time.

3. Add melted unsweetened chocolate.

4. Add cake flour and baking soda.

5. Add buttermilk and vanilla extract.

6. Add chocolate chips.

Place cupcake liner into pans and fill each cup with 1 leveled off scoop of an ice cream scooper. Bake at 350 degrees in the oven for 20-25 minutes or until tester comes out clean.

Chocolate Butter Cream Frosting

INGREDIENTS

3 sticks unsalted butter, (softened)
1 cup unsweetened cocoa (sifted)
5 cups confectioner's sugar (sifted)
1/2 cup milk
2 teaspoons vanilla extract
1/2 teaspoon salt

DIRECTIONS

1. Cream the butter for few minutes in a mixer with the paddle attachment on medium speed.
2. Add sifted cocoa and sugar and turn on the mixer on the lowest speed. until the sugar and cocoa are absorbed by the butter.
3. Increase mixer speed to medium and add milk, vanilla extract, salt and beat for 3 minutes. If your frosting needs a stiffer consistency, add a little more sugar. If your frosting needs to be thinned out, add additional milk 1 tablespoon at a time.

*Recipes by Purple Elephant Cakes
www.PurpleElephantCakes.com
www.SmallGoodsMarket.com

Made in the USA
Monee, IL
13 May 2022